Leslie Baker

MORNING BEACH

Little, Brown and Company
Boston Toronto London

Also illustrated by Leslie Baker

THE THIRD-STORY CAT by Leslie Baker
WINTER HARVEST by Jane Chelsea Aragon

First edition

Library of Congress Cataloging-in-Publication Data

Baker, Leslie A.
  Morning beach / Leslie Baker. — 1st ed.
    p.   cm.
  Summary: Relates a young girl's early morning trip to the ocean
with her mother on the first day of summer vacation.
  ISBN 0-316-07835-2
  [1. Seashore — Fiction. 2. Vacations — Fiction.]   I. Title.
PZ7.B1744Mo 1989
[E] — dc19   88–25836
                                                      CIP
                                                       AC

10 9 8 7 6 5 4 3 2 1

Published simultaneously in Canada
by Little, Brown & Company (Canada) Limited

Printed in the United States of America

To Ken, who remembers another morning beach

A patch of summer sun warms my face, awakening me. It is early, and for a while I snuggle back into my soft quilt. But then I remember we are at Grandma's.

I throw back the covers and jump out of bed. Today is the first day of my summer vacation. This morning Mom and I are going to the beach. Every year we take the first trip together by ourselves. Grandma took Mom when she was a little girl.

I dress quickly. The morning air feels cool against my bare feet and legs as I tiptoe downstairs.

Sunlight fills the kitchen, where Mom is packing my favorite lunch. I gulp my cereal, watching her wrap the peanut butter sandwiches, oatmeal cookies, and apple juice we always take. There is barely room for the fat peaches she has left for last.

After breakfast we look in Grandma's closet for the things we put away last summer. On one shelf I see Grandma's shells and Mom's collection of pink beach stones. On another are my bug net, dragon kite, and pinwheel. For the trip I take my knapsack and an old pail and shovel. Mom pulls out her favorite sun hat.

Outside, the wet grass tickles my legs as we head for the shed where our bikes are stored. Mom's bike still has my old baby seat on it.

Finally we pedal off as the sun begins to burn away the morning chill.

We ride down our quiet lane, past sleeping houses. One, two, three, four, five I count, pointing to each in turn. I remember the names of the children who live there. We will have all summer long to play hide-and-seek together.

We hear a dog bark. He chases us up the road, and I pedal faster, scared, until I see his happy eyes and panting smile.

It is Ben's dog, Moe. He only wants a friend to play with on this country road. He dances around my spinning wheels until the road starts to climb. Then he turns back and woofs a good-bye.

I pump harder now, trailing Mom up the steep hill. My hair sticks to my cheeks as each push brings me closer to the top. I can already taste the treat my mom always buys me there.

The store is almost empty, except for a man looking at the newspapers and two fishermen buying cold drinks. I run over to pet Lambert, the grumpy Maine coon cat. I know he remembers me from last year, but he pretends he doesn't.

We sit on the steps and eat our Popsicles. I always choose red, and Mom always picks orange. It is so cold and good my mouth feels frozen, even after the hot ride. The ice melts, and our hands get sticky. Mom and I giggle. Popsicles for breakfast!

Soon we are off again. I race along faster and faster. I pretend my bike is a horse galloping through meadows. The trees and fields blur as the wind cools my face.

Mom pedals along more slowly. I slip behind her as she points out the wildflowers that grow in this field. Every year I remember more names.

I'm tired now, but we're almost there. We just have to go past the pond where the turtles always sun themselves.

As usual, Mr. Pender is taking his morning swim with an inner tube tied around his waist. Sometimes he gets tired and just sits for a while, floating in the middle of the pond.

I am the first to spot the path, where we will leave our bikes and start to walk. I can hardly wait to see the ocean.

But this year the path is closed. Our special trip is ruined. I almost
start to cry.

Then Mom remembers another path she took with Grandma long ago. I help her search for it, but I don't see anything.

She thinks she spots it down the road, near the stone wall. Together we push away the tangle of vines. We've uncovered the old trail.

The woods are quiet and dark. It's a little scary, but Mom takes my hand. She tells me how she used to pretend to be one of the Indians who once walked in these woods. We try to move silently as I search the ground for arrowheads.

I see something on the path. It is a beautiful black stone covered with white stripes. Right there, I decide to start my own collection this summer. It will be like Mom's and Grandma's, but mine will be only special striped stones.

As I put the stone away, I notice the path has become sandy. The beach is just ahead. Without waiting for Mom, I run out into the open, kick my sneakers off, and scramble up the dunes. The soft sand slides beneath my feet, daring me to reach the top. "Almost there, almost there," I sing under my breath.

I'm there! Dropping my pack, I spread my arms and sail down the bare dunes to the sea.

Mom stays behind for a moment and watches me from above. I run as fast as I can on this morning beach. My footprints fill with water, leaving the first tracks of the day behind me.

D